I SPY SHAVUOT
BOOK FOR KIDS

THIS BOOK BELONGS TO:

_____

it is some yummy
CHEESE CAKE

I spy with my little eye something that starts with

T

it is the holy
TORAH

it is a bunch of pretty FLOWERS

I SPY with my Little eye Something that STARTS with

it is the brave
KING DAVID

I SPY with my Little eye
Something that Starts with

IT IS THE HOLY
MOUNT SINAI

IT IS A BIG FRUIT BASKET

I SPY with my little eye Something that starts with

it is some delicious
ICE CREAM

I SPY WITH MY LITTLE EYE
SOMETHING THAT STARTS WITH

M

IT IS THE HOLY
MOSES

I spy with my little eye something that starts with C

it is the ten
COMMANDMENTS

IT IS A SHINY TORAH
CROWN

I SPY with my Little eye Something that Starts with B

it is some hot cheese
BLINTZES

I SPY with my Little eye Something that STARTS with R

it is the beautiful
RUTH

I SPY with my Little eye
Something that Starts with

it is some crunchy
WHEAT

it is some cold
MILK

See all the "I Spy" Jewish Holiday Books for Kids from the Publisher

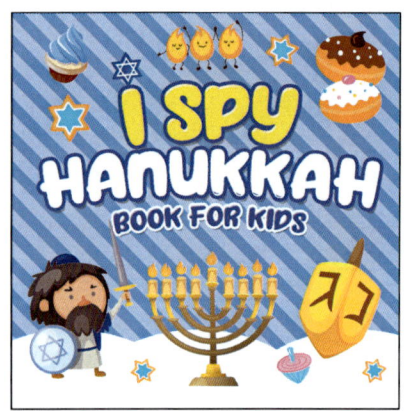
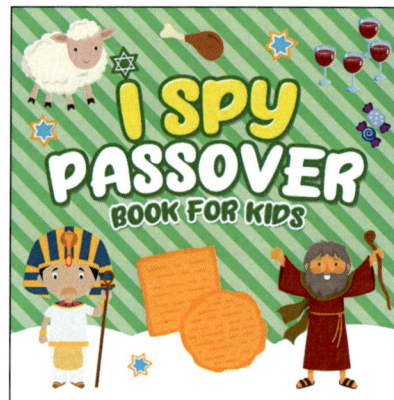
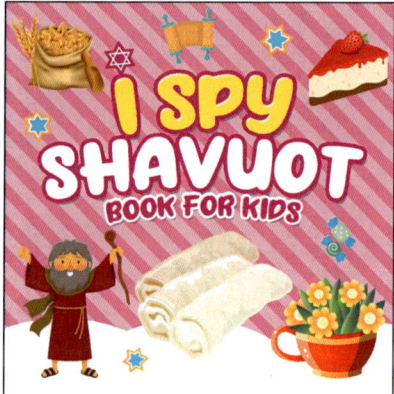

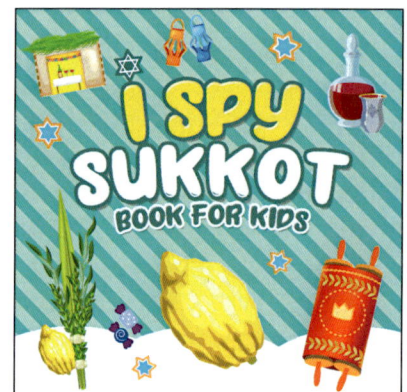
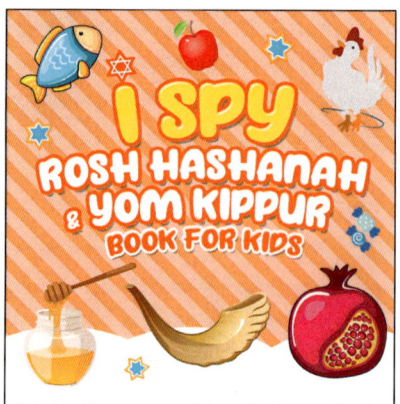

WE WOULD LOVE TO HEAR FROM YOU!

Kindly take a few minutes of your time to leave a review online at the website you purchased this book!

SCAN HERE

View more information and to purchase other books in this series and other educational books by Jewish Learning Press

Made in United States
North Haven, CT
27 May 2025